CARTOON NETWORK™

SCOOBY-DOO!™

FALL FRIGHT

By Gail Herman
illustrated by Duendes del Sur

SCHOLASTIC INC.
New York   Toronto   London   Auckland
Sydney   Mexico City   New Delhi   Hong Kong

ISBN 978-0-439-78358-3

Illustrations by Duendes del Sur

13 12 11   11 12 13 14 15/0

Printed in the U.S.A.   40
First printing, September 2005

It was a windy, stormy fall day in Coolsville.
B-r-r-i-i-ng! B-r-r-i-i-n-g!
Scooby-Doo picked up the telephone.
"Rello?"
"Hello?"
Shaggy put his ear close to the phone, too.

"Hi guys!" said Velma. "Daphne and Fred are here. Come over, too. We'll stay inside and eat pizza."

"Staying inside? Eating pizza? Like, you read our minds," said Shaggy. "Scoob and I will bring videos and dessert."

"Hurry!" Velma told them.

Shaggy and Scooby stepped outside. The wind blew them back in.

"Like, we need some outerwear, good buddy," said Shaggy.

Outside, raindrops began to fall.
"Let's go to Shaun and Ted's Video Store!"
Shaggy shouted to Scooby above the wind.
"It's just around the corner."

"Roughnuts rirst?" asked Scooby.
"Of course, doughnuts first," Shaggy agreed.
"We'll get dessert, then choose movies."

A few minutes later, they left the shop.
"Like, care for a cruller?" Shaggy opened
the box. A gust of wind knocked it over.
"Rotcha!" Scooby cried, diving for the
doughnuts.

Shaggy caught a chocolate frosted,
a cinnamon bun, and a double fudge
delight — right in his mouth!

"I never thought I'd say this, Scoob,"
he mumbled, "but let's cool it on the
crullers. It's way too windy."

Next they went to the candy store . . .
then the bakery . . . and finally, the ice
cream shop!

The skies were dark now. Branches bent in
the wind. Rain splattered the sidewalk.
　　"We'd better hurry, good buddy," said Shaggy.
"To Shaun and Ted's!"

The friends hurried to the video store. Spooky light spilled onto the sidewalk. "Zoinks!" said Shaggy. He screeched to a stop by the door. "This place isn't Shaun and Ted's Videos. It's Haunted Videos!"

Shaggy and Scooby looked at the sign. They looked at each other. They ran. But they didn't get far.

"Ahhh!" screamed Shaggy.

A cold wet hand came out of nowhere.
It covered his face.
"Help! I can't see!"
The hand fell away, and Shaggy shivered.
"Like, this place really is haunted," he
cried. "Go, Scooby, go!"

But where could they go? They ran this way, and that. Everywhere they went, they saw ghosts whirling around!

Scooby peered down the street.

"Ronster!" he shouted.

"Monster? You mean *ghost*, good buddy," Shaggy shouted back.

"Ro ray!" Scooby pointed. "Ronster!"

Now Shaggy saw it, too. A monster. Coming toward them, big and fast, rumbling closer and closer.

Shaggy and Scooby froze in fear. There was no escape.

"Scooby! Shaggy!" it called out.

"Like, it knows our names!" said Shaggy. "Of course we know your names." Fred stuck his head from the side of the monster. "Fred's been swallowed!" Shaggy cried.

"What are you talking about?" Daphne stuck her head out, too. "We're driving the Mystery Machine. You two were taking so long at the store, we came to find you!"

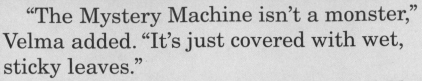

"The Mystery Machine isn't a monster," Velma added. "It's just covered with wet, sticky leaves."

"But what about the ghosts?" asked Shaggy.

Just then, a gust of wind blew through the street.

"Ghosts?!" said Velma. "Those
are just leaves. The wind is blowing
them in spooky shapes!"

"But a ghost slapped me in the face!" said Shaggy.

"Like this?" Velma took a hand-shaped leaf and held it up to Shaggy's face.

"Uh, uh, yeah," Shaggy agreed. "But what about . . ."

"Raunted Videos?" Scooby reminded him.
"That's right!" exclaimed Shaggy. "The
video store! It's haunted! Come on!"

Shaggy led everyone to the door.
"See? It says HAUNTED."
Velma picked sticky leaves off the sign.
"It's still Shaun and Ted's. Some letters
got covered. That's all."

"There aren't any ghosts or monsters,"
Fred told them. "It's just the rain and wind."
"There's nothing to be afraid of," Daphne
added. "And besides, the storm is letting up."

27

All at once, Shaggy's face turned white.
Scooby's jaw dropped in fear. "Roh no!"
"Like, this is the scariest thing yet!"
Shaggy cried. "It's terrible! It's horrible!"

"What is it?" cried Velma.

"We dropped the desserts!" Shaggy moaned.

Shoppings bags were trampled. Boxes lay smashed on the ground. The ice cream, candy, doughnuts, and pies were ruined!

"It's too late to get more," wailed Shaggy. "All the stores are closed!"

"Well, at least the video store is open," said Fred.

Shaggy and Scooby raced inside. "Here they are!" said Shaggy.

He pulled video after video from the shelf:
Make Your Own Desserts, Part 1,
Make Your Own Desserts, Part 2,
and *Make Your Own Desserts, Part 3.*

"We saved the day, Scoob!" said Shaggy.

"Scooby-Dooby-Doo!" Scooby howled.